Pig Is Big on Books

DOUGLAS FLORIAN

Holiday House / New York

In memory of Diane Florian

Copyright © 2015 by Douglas Florian
All Rights Reserved
HOLIDAY HOUSE is registered in the U.S. Patent and Trademark Office.
Printed and Bound in April 2015 at Tien Wah Press, Johor Bahru, Johor, Malaysia.
The artwork was created with gouache watercolor, colored pencil and
collage on primed paper bag.
www.holidayhouse.com
First Edition
1 3 5 7 9 10 8 6 4 2

Library of Congress Cataloging-in-Publication Data
Florian, Douglas, author, illustrator.
Pig is big on books / Douglas Florian. — First edition.
pages cm. — (I like to read)
Summary: Pig loves books, both big and small, and
reads them at school, at home, and on the bus.
ISBN 978-0-8234-3393-3 (hardcover)
[1. Books and reading—Fiction. 2. Pigs—Fiction.] I. Title.
PZ7.F6645Pi 2015
[E]—dc23
2014032162

ISBN 978-0-8234-3424-4 (paperback)

Pig is big on books.

Pig likes to read.

Pig reads big books.

Pig reads small books.

Pig reads at home.

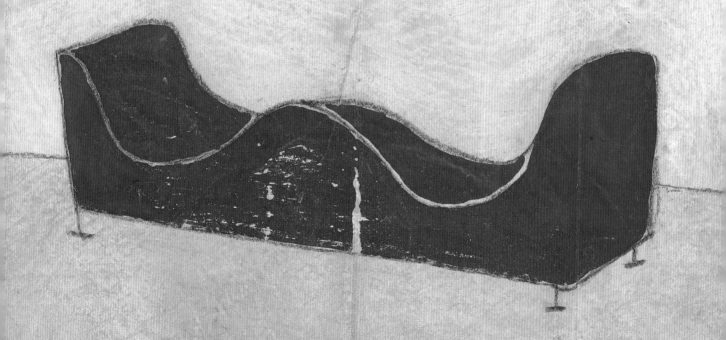

Pig reads at school.

Pig reads on the bus.

Pig reads with Cat.

And Pig reads with his mom.

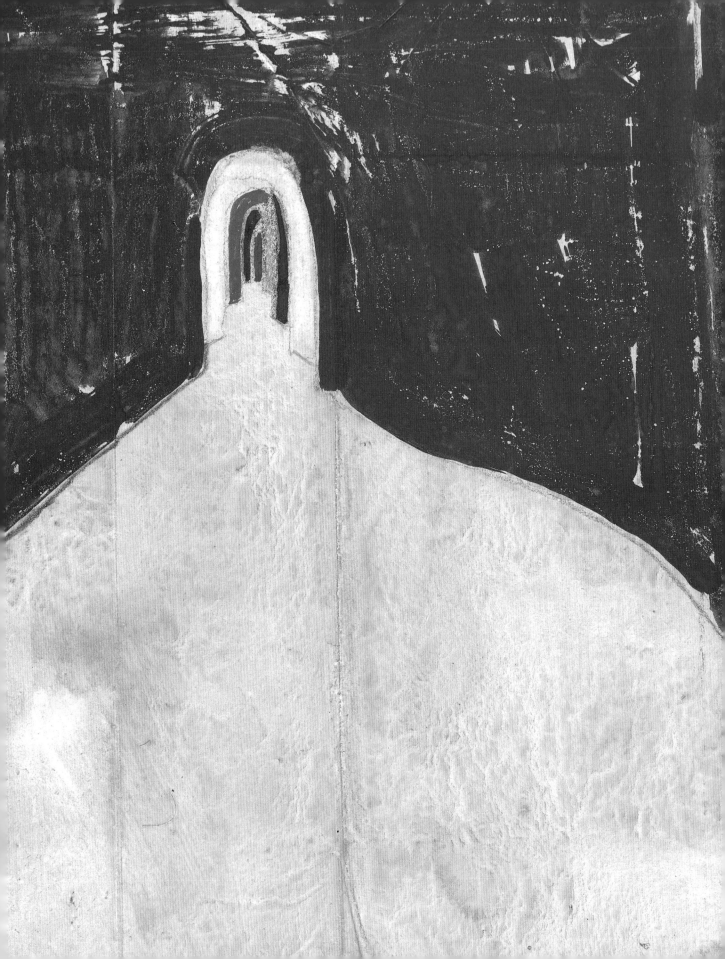

One day pig had no books.

Pig looked and looked.

He did not find even one book.

So Pig wrote a book.

Pig wrote **this** book.